Acting Edition

Harry Clarke

by David Cale

FOR PRODUCTION INQUIRIES

UNITED STATES AND CANADA
info@concordtheatricals.com
1-866-979-0447

UNITED KINGDOM AND EUROPE
licensing@concordtheatricals.co.uk
020-7054-7298

Each title is subject to availability from Concord Theatricals Corp., depending upon country of performance. Please be aware that *HARRY CLARKE* may not be licensed by Concord Theatricals Corp. in your territory. Professional and amateur producers should contact the nearest Concord Theatricals Corp. office or licensing partner to verify availability.

HARRY CLARKE was first produced in New York City by the Vineyard Theatre (Douglas Aibel, Artistic Director; Sarah Stern, Artistic Director; Suzanne Appel, Managing Director) in 2017. The play was subsequently produced Off Broadway in 2018 by Audible at the Minetta Lane Theatre, New York City. The artistic team for both productions included: scenic design by Alexander Dodge, costumer design by Kaye Voyce, lighting design by Alan C. Edwards, and sound design by Bart Fasbender. The director was Leigh Silverman, and original songs were by David Cale. The cast was as follows for both productions:

PHILIP BRUGGLESTEIN / HARRY CLARKE . . . . Billy Crudup

CHARACTERS

PHILIP BRUGGLESTEIN / HARRY CLARKE

A single deck chair stands on a bare stage.

Low-key yet tantalizing cinematic music plays, like the opening credits music for a mystery movie or a thriller.[*]

The music fades.

Philip Brugglestein walks out.

A curiously captivating but essentially timid man from the Midwest, Philip feels more himself speaking with an English accent.

His self-confidence fully comes alive when adopting the persona of a cocky Londoner, Harry Clarke.

He addresses the audience with an English accent, but when he recalls what people from his past have said he replicates their American voices and demeanors with uncanny accuracy, almost as if he's able to channel the personalities of the people he's recalling.

I could always do an immaculate English accent.

Ever since I was a little kid. I don't know where it came from. English TV shows on PBS? English movies?

I don't remember much about my childhood, but I remember laying out on the football field at school in South Bend, Indiana with this kid from my class, Chris Keane, and saying,

"I could be myself if I had an English accent."

---

*A license to produce *Harry Clarke* does not include a performance license for any third-party or copyrighted cinematic music. Licensees should create an original composition or use music in the public domain. For further information, please see Music Use Note on page iii.

And Chris Keane staring at me blankly, not saying a word, but me knowing that I had just uncovered what would be one of the fundamental truths of my life.

My mom died when I was fifteen and my dad died just before my eighteenth birthday. After he died I went through all his possessions. Came across an 8mm film that in four minutes crystallizes my whole childhood.

The film was taken just after my mom and dad and I moved from Evanston to South Bend. Somebody had given my dad a camera and tripod and this was his one attempt at using it.

In the film my father is interviewing me in the front yard. I'm about eight years old at the time.

He says to me, "What do you think of the new house, Phil?"

My name was Philip Brugglestein then.

I answer, "Oh, it's lovely, Father."

I was posher then.

My dad yells out, "Lois, he's speakin' in that goddamn English accent again!"

My mother comes into the shot and says, "Don't upset your father."

I say, "But it's my real voice."

And my dad loses it.

"Phil, you're an American! You were born in Illinois. No one in this family has ever been to Europe. You don't stop talking in that Britty Brit accent I'm takin' you to the doctor. He says you need electroshock to cure you, I'm going to let him plug you into the goddamn wall! You want to get electrocuted huh? Huh?"

My mother starts screaming, "Jack, don't scare him!"

I'm yelling, "It's my voice, Mummy. I cant help how I sound!"

My father hollers, "You wanted to keep the kid, you deal with this."

Storms off.

My mother runs after him and in the background of the 8mm film you hear,

"What the hell's that supposed to mean? Don't you ever talk like that in front of him. You're a pig. I cannot wait to leave you. Why was I thinking it was going to be any different when we moved to Indiana? ...Don't you raise a finger with me."

They're battling it out in the kitchen. I'm left standing alone in front of the camera, which is still running, and I start clowning around doing this character I'd come up with – Harry Clarke.

I'm eight years old looking into the camera and going,

"'Allo! My name's Harry Clarke.

You awright?

Don't get your knickers in a twist, darlin'.

Why these people yellin' all the time?

Come off it.

They're bonkers.

I feel like I'm livin' in a bloody mad house.

I'm Harry Clarke, and I'm gonna mess you up.

'Cause I'm Harry Clarke.

Yeah!"

> *He pulls a comical, child-like Harry Clarke face to the camera.*

My dad comes into the frame, goes, "And you wanna know why you get kicked around at school!"

Whaps me on the side of the head and the screen goes blank.

After my father's funeral I donated the contents of our house to Goodwill, put the house on the market, and when I found a buyer, took the money and walked away from

Indiana. I got on a plane to New York, and from the day I landed only spoke with an English accent.

If anyone asked where I was from, I told them I was from Elstree, north of London, where the film studios are.

I felt liberated. Special. I felt like I was finally being myself.

When I got into my thirties, I thought of levelling with people about where I came from. To test the water I told one person I know who moved to the West Coast. We don't have any friends in common. He had such an adverse response. "I'll never see you in the same light. I'll never see you the same way." He stopped returning my calls. I thought, I'm not telling anyone else. All my friends in New York know me as an English person. The Evanston and South Bend years seem like such a thing of the past. Irrelevant to me now. So I'm just gonna leave things as they are, get on with my life.

And I didn't think about Harry Clarke for years.

Till one day he re-appeared.

He sits on the chair.

It was a strange time. I wasn't working. Didn't know what to do with myself.

He speaks confidingly to the audience.

I was wandering around midtown Manhattan. Sixth Avenue and 49th Street. There was a guy walking ahead of me. And I don't know why I did this, or what made me choose to do it with him, but I thought, I'm going to follow that guy. See where he goes.

He walks south on Sixth Avenue.

I trail behind him.

This must be what a stalker feels like. Or a private detective or a cop.

He crosses the avenue at 48th.

I do the same.

He ducks into The Gap.

I follow him into the store. He picks up four packs of grey boxer briefs. There's a large sign above them. "Special Sale. Two packs of two for twenty dollars."

I hang near the jeans while he stands on line to pay, and when he leaves the store I follow him south, and then west along 46th Street, keeping about thirty feet behind.

Where are we headed? I think. Where are you leading me?

He goes into the Dean and DeLuca in the lobby of the Paramount Hotel. I wait a few moments and follow him inside.

When I get up to the counter he's paying for an iced coffee. I order an espresso and sit at the empty table next to him.

He reaches into his pocket for a little pill container. Takes two white tablets out of it. I can't read what the label says. Washes them down with iced coffee, and gets on his phone.

I hear him say, "Sabine, I don't want to go to couples counseling. I've made the decision... Sabine, Sabine, you're not listening to me, it's over."

Then he says a few sentences in French and the call ends, as though this Sabine had hung up on him.

He dials another number.

I hear him say, "Jed, hey. Look, I got some family stuff I have to attend to unexpectedly. I'm not coming back to the office. Gonna head back to Connecticut."

When he hangs up I think to myself, what are you doing? Get out of here. Leave!

On the street I figure, no harm done. He had no idea I was following him. I just got a little glimpse into somebody's life. I won't do it again. It was just my morning for doing something I'd never done before. Now I know what it's like to follow a stranger around.

A few months later I go to see a play in a little theatre in Tribeca. The lights come up for intermission. The person sitting across the aisle from me looks familiar. I'm thinking, where do I know that face from? I know you from somewhere, and I realize it's the guy that I'd followed that day.

And I must have been staring at him as I tried to figure out who he was because when I came out of my head he was glaring at me.

And without thinking I squint up my eyes and say, "Sorry, I didn't mean to stare but I think we've met before. With Sabine?"

"Oh yeah," he says, trying to make it seem like he remembers. "What's your name again?"

I feel a surge of panic. What the hell am I going to say? Paralyzed for a moment then oddly calm. It's like another force is pulling me out of my seat towards him. I get up, look him in the eye, extend my hand and say,

"I'm Harry Clarke. What's your name again?"

> *From this point on every time Philip interacts with Mark Schmidt he speaks in Harry's voice, and every time he recalls what Mark says it's in Mark's faintly Long Island accent.*

"Mark Schmidt."

"Pleased to re-meet you Mark Schmidt. You enjoying the play?"

"It's unusual to be in the theatre and feel tension."

"This play's like a mystery. In that sense, seems more like a movie. You on your own?"

"Yes, I couldn't find anyone to come with me. My friend's on the board of the theatre. Wanted to be supportive. It got a very good review."

"I'm sorry, I don't understand why anyone would read reviews. Why would you want to know what's going to happen? Isn't one of the powers of art rooted in the element of surprise?

I remember years ago seeing that film Sexy Beast. I didn't know a thing about it. From the title I assumed it must be one of those soft-core porn films the English are partial to. But it was nothing at all as I imagined. All these former criminals laying low in Spain. It was fabulous. But part of what made it great for me was I knew absolutely nothing about it. The impact of the film was connected to the unknown."

"I'm guessing by your accent, you're from London?"

"Could you tell? Wish I could remember where we met. I don't know why I'm thinking it was Connecticut."

"I used to live in Stamford. When I was with Sabine. I was going to get a drink. Can I get you something?"

"Oh, thanks. Whatever you're having. Surprise me."

He comes back from the concessions stand. Hands me a drink.

"Sabine and I separated."

"I'm sorry."

"I moved into Manhattan. Sabine's talking about moving back to Paris. I hope she does. I'd be happy if I never run into her again. You married?"

"Nah, never met the right bird."

"Bird?"

"Girl, chick, woman. Funny how the English call girls, 'birds.' And the Americans call 'em 'chicks.' Wonder where all this avian terminology hails from? Wine's pretty good for something that comes in a plastic cup."

The lights begin flickering. We take our seats. I can't concentrate on the second half of the play. I feel like I've had an out of body experience. Harry Clarke was a character I did for myself. Harry Clarke had never made an appearance in New York. I'll make a quick exit at the end of the show. Don't need to talk to the guy again.

But there's a bottleneck of people at the front of the theatre and coming from directly behind me I hear,

"I can see why you don't read reviews, Harry. Wish I hadn't known the brother wasn't who he said he was."

I turn back, and Harry Clarke kicks in again.

"I could eat a fucking pony. I'm going to get something to eat, you wanna join me?"

"You know, I haven't eaten since this morning."

"Come on, you gotta eat."

Walking through the street I notice my walk has changed. My posture is different. I'm standing up straight. I seem to have a whole new internal life.

We go to a fish restaurant. After we order he asks me what I do for a living.

A slight pause of hesitation.

"Right now, nothing. Unemployed. But for the last twenty years, up till last year, I was tour manager slash personal assistant slash whatever-else-was-needed type person for a recording artist in England."

"Anyone I might know?"

And just one word flies into my brain, out through my mouth and makes its home in the world.

"Sade."

"Sade! Oh man, how cool! What's she like?"

"Well, she's about the most real person I know. What's she like? She's funny. Loyal. Kind. Extremely astute about people emotionally. Little bit of a recluse. You have to pull her out of her shell sometimes. I was with her for twenty years. One of my closest friends at this point. Though I can't say I've seen her much of late. When I left the job I felt I needed to shake things up in my life, so I got on a plane and here I am. What d'you do?"

"Building appraisals for banks and insurance companies, not very interesting. Sometimes, I feel there's a more adventurous, artistic person inside me wriggling to get out."

"Oh, let 'im out. Give 'im the run of the place."

"Easy to say. I realized recently, I have such a recognizable life, it's interchangeable with any number of people. An indistinct life."

"My life's had no planning. It's an intuitive trail that goes where it wants to go. I feel like fate is pulling me along. I happen to meet Sade in a pub in East London when she was just getting started, that led to what that became. I happen to meet you in Connecticut, now here we are."

"Wish I could have more of a connection to the arts. I think about producing movies. I know people with money. I could find investors. But then everyone tells me, you can't make money in independent films, so I back off."

"You gotta get a little ballsy sometimes. Find a script you like and just throw yourself into it."

"I need to be around more people like you, Harry. Everyone I know is so cautious. They would never get up and move to another country because they wanted a change."

"I thought, England doesn't suit me right now. I need to feel like a stranger in town. So here I am. A stranger in a strange land. Some people live their lives so seriously. I'm having fun with mine."

We keep talking and polish off two bottles of wine, and he says,

"Look, my place is literally four blocks from here. I have this potato vodka from Lithuania. Come back and I'll make you a nightcap that'll put color in your dreams."

"Sure", I say.

We stand up to leave. He slaps me on the shoulder.

"You're a cool guy, Harry Clarke."

His apartment is on the eleventh floor of a new building in Tribeca overlooking the river. He mixes us the strongest martini I've ever had in my life and asks me what my honest take on Sabine is. I tell him I only met her once.

"I'll tell you this, I had a lot more hang-ups after our relationship than I had going into it."

I ask him what he means.

"Suddenly in the middle of making love she'd say something like, 'Mark, don't do that with your tongue.' I'd say, 'Do what?' She'd say, 'You're making your tongue go hard when you kiss me, I don't like it.' I'd say, 'I have no idea what you're talking about, Sabine.' She'd say, 'Well just keep your tongue soft.' For weeks after, every time we were intimate, I'd be crippled with self-consciousness.

Or she'd say, 'You're so tender and sensitive I feel like I'm having sex with another woman. That we're a pair of lesbians.'

Then she got into this whole gay thing with me. I can't believe I'm telling you this shit. It's the potato vodka and the tempranillo talking.

Oh, she'd say, 'I feel like I'm with a man who never really explored who he is sexually.' She'd say, 'Ask Fred.' We had this gay friend Fred. 'Call him up. Ask him if he'll come over and fuck you next time I'm in France. Tell him I give him my blessing. He'll wear a condom. You won't catch anything. You're blushing!' 'Of course I'm blushing, Sabine,' I'd say, 'I'm embarrassed for you.' I'm making another drink. You havin' one?"

"Why not?" I say, trying to say as little as possible so he wouldn't be able to tell I was having trouble keeping my words from sliding into one another.

We finish up the martinis. He glances at his watch. "Man I have to be up in four hours. Gotta go to bed."

Five minutes later I'm in the back of a cab hurtling up the FDR thinking, that was the weirdest night of my life. What the hell were you doing?

I wake up groggy and dehydrated. Pick up my jeans off the floor and a business card falls out.

Mark Schmidt
Vice President
Redman Appraisals.

I remember I'd given him my home phone number and that my name is on the outgoing message of the answering machine. So before I have coffee I change it to simply, "Please leave a message."

By late afternoon the whole thing is off my mind. I'm drifting in and out of a Raymond Chandler short story, when the home phone rings.

Coming out of the answering machine I hear,

"Harry Clarke! Mark Schmidt here. So much fun last night. Hey look, man, tell me if you're not up for this, my folks have a boat they keep up in Rhode Island and my mom's a huge Sade fan and my sister's a singer-songwriter and my mom wants to meet you and my dad wants my sister to play you some of her songs, have you give her your professional advice. They're up in Newport right now. And they invited us to spend the weekend on the boat. I know I hardly know you..."

I lunge at the phone.

"Mark Schmidt – star of last night. Yeah, I'd love to come to Rhode Island."

"You know I could take Friday off and we could get a head start on the weekend."

"Sounds groovy. I'll swing by your apartment. Ten a.m. Friday morning, okay?"

I put down the phone and it's like a fever flaring up. I go to the computer. Do a search for the names of travel agents in London. Write down the number of one and dial it. Get the after-hours answering machine with a brief message. Hanging up, I program the travel agent's number into my phone. List it as *Sade – Home*.

The next few days I read everything I can get my hands on about Sade. Every interview. Every profile.

And on Friday morning Mark Schmidt and Harry Clarke are heading north up I-95.

"Harry, I gotta warn you, my dad seems like a tough guy, but he's all heart. Don't let him intimidate you. He's actually in bad health. Doesn't have much longer, though you'd never know it. Oh, and my mom has really big hair. I don't know, the older she gets the bigger she seems to like it. You're gonna think it's a wig. It's not a wig."

The ride takes five hours and we pull into a parking lot in Newport. Walk to the harbour.

"There's The Jewish American Princess."

"The what?"

"The Jewish American Princess, it's the name of the boat," pointing at what must have been a several million dollar yacht.

Whoah, I think, we are in the land of serious money.

Mrs. Schmidt greets us. Her hair *is* huge.

> *When recalling what the Schmidt family says*
> *he adopts their voices.*

She throws her arms around me and says, "I'm gonna hug you, even though I don't know you."

Mr. Schmidt shakes my hand and doesn't say a whole lot.

Below deck, the spare bedroom looks like a mini hotel room.

Mark says, "I'll take the floor. I brought a sleeping bag with me."

I feel like an imposter, I feel like someone who's broken into someone's home, till fifteen minutes later when we start hitting the cocktails. I'd never seen people drink like it, and Harry takes to holding court.

"I'm gonna get Sade on the phone."

Mrs. Schmidt says, "I can't believe this!"

I take out the phone. Lay it on the table and program in *Sade*. Mrs. Schmidt's eyes are glued to the little screen. Up comes, *Sade Home* and the English phone number. I press *Call*, get up from the table and pace.

> *He gets up and mimes the phone conversation to illustrate the story.*

On the other end of the phone I hear,

> *Spoken in a clipped English accent.*

"You have reached the offices of Blackburn Travel."

"Oh damn. It's gone to voicemail."

> *In a clipped English accent.*

"The office is closed. If you'd like to leave a message, one of our representatives will call you back in the morning. Thank you. Beep!"

"Hey Sade, it's Harry. I'm on a boat off Rhode Island in America, if you can believe, with some friends of mine, and I was just thinking about you. Thought I'd give you a call, see how you are."

Everyone on the deck is riveted. I look over at Mark's mother.

"You want to say something to Sade?"

> *Into the phone.*

"My friend, Mrs. Schmidt, wants to say hello."

> *He hands her the phone.*

"Sade, hi! Ruth Schmidt here. We love your music. Thank you for all the pleasure you've given us over the years, and we're really enjoying Soldier of Love. Take care, Sade."

> *She hands back the phone.*

"Alright, love, look after yourself. Try you another time. Big kiss."

> *He hangs up.*

Mrs. Schmidt goes off like a firework. "Oh my God I have to call Peggy!"

She gets on her phone.

"Peggy, I just left a message on Sade's answering machine... How many people are called Sade, Peggy? Yes, Sade Sade!"

Mark leans into me. "Thanks, man, you've just made her year."

I lean into him and whisper, "Your mom's very sweet."

And as I do it my lower lip brushes his ear. And I think, that was a bit of alright. So I do it again.

"Your dad's nice too."

Stephanie Schmidt arrives in the late afternoon. Mid-thirties. Bright red hair. Carrying a beaten-up guitar case. I think, this is going to be excruciating. Like one of those American Idol auditions.

On the deck of the boat, she takes out the guitar. Begins to slap it.

Stephanie sings.

"I FOUND A CONDOM IN YOUR CAR
I FOUND A CONDOM IN YOUR CAR
I FOUND A CONDOM IN YOUR CAR
SO YES IT'S OVER."

Mrs. Schmidt jumps up.

"Stephanie, we have boat neighbors, please! Enough with the condoms!"

Stephanie rolls her eyes, says, "Why don't I just play Harry a track on the headphones?" Sets me up with a song called, "He's Coming Over to Paint Me." It's a ballad. Plain and real. I try to encourage her. She isn't particularly interested in a career.

"I write songs because it gives me pleasure. And because it expresses something for me. When I'm writing I have a different energy. People always seem to gravitate towards me more when I'm being artistic."

Mr. Schmidt says, "Give Harry a copy of your CD, maybe he can play it for Sade."

And I feel embarrassed, and wretched, and small.

The rest of the day is a rolling sea of dirty martinis.

In the evening Mark and I go into the bedroom, by this point both of us are drunk. He pulls out the sleeping bag. Unfolds it on the floor.

"That's ridiculous, you can't sleep on the floor. Lay up here on the bed. What's the big deal?"

He gathers up the sleeping bag. Lays it on top of the bed.

"Dude, it's eighty-five degrees, you don't need the sleeping bag, you just need a sheet. Don't be such a girl, get in the bed. I want to go to sleep."

"I'm just your little bitch, aren't I?"

"Yeah, you are, and don't make me have to slap you around."

"Oooooh."

I slap his ass.

"Get in the fucking bed."

He gets on the top and pulls the sheet over him, turning his back to me.

"Night, honey bunny."

"Nighty night, sweetheart."

He falls asleep quickly.

I can't sleep, so I get up, leave the boat and go for a walk around Newport at night. Find a little gay bar, one of the few things still open. Go in and sit up the bar with a drink. There's a kid sitting on his own perched along from me. We catch each other's eyes.

He says, "I couldn't get to sleep."

I mouth, "Me neither."

The place is quiet then some music comes on.

> *We hear Sade's "Hang On To Your Love"*
> *coming over the sound system.*
>
> *As the song plays, we hear Harry's side of the*
> *conversation, and with a shift of the lights we*
> *are in the bar.*

Hey, you wanna dance?

Come on, let's dance.

> *The guitar part enters the song, Harry dances*
> *with the music, and when he speaks it is in*
> *synch with the track.*

My name's Harry.

Yeah, I'm English.

> *He dances without speaking as we hear Sade*
> *sing:*

> "In heaven's name, why are you walking away?
> Hang on to your love
> In heaven's name, why do you play these games?
> Hang on to your love..."

> *He dances, and leans in to the kid, as if to let*
> *him speak into his ear, and then leans back*
> *out.*

Just visiting. My wife and I are staying with my friend on
his boat.

She's asleep. I couldn't sleep so I went for a walk. Here I
am.

What's your name?

Luke?

Luke, you're very cute. I'm direct, fuck it.

> *They dance.*

> *Harry leans in to the kid to hear him better.*

We live in Camden.

Where d'you live?

You still live with your mom and dad. That's cool.

What's my wife's name? Why do you want to know what my wife's name is?

Sabine. Her name's Sabine. She's French. Français. I met her in Paris.

What am I doing in a gay bar? Dancing. What are you doing in a gay bar, Sunshine?

Yeah, I bet you are.

> *Sade sings: "Hang on to your love."*
>
> *The song abruptly stops, lights shift, and we are out of the bar.*

I come out of the bathroom. Close the door as quietly as I can.

Mark turns over under the sheet.

"Where d'you go?"

"I went for a walk."

"Shower woke me up."

"It's hot outside. I took a shower. I'm sorry I woke you up."

I get into the bed.

"My sister likes you."

"I like your sister too. Go back to sleep."

My face is facing his back. I can smell the laundry detergent on his T-shirt. I'm breathing it in. And I suddenly feel I've got on a ride I cannot get off.

> *We hear a blast of urgent violins.* *The kind of music that would underscore a danger point in a movie thriller.*

---

*A license to produce *Harry Clarke* does not include a performance license for any third-party or copyrighted violin music. Licensees should create an original composition or use music in the public domain. For further information, please see Music Use Note on page iii.

After a few moments, the music level lowers and underscores.

On the deck of the boat Mark taps me on the shoulder,

"What are you listening to?"

Harry removes headphones and switches his iPod off. The music stops.

"Soundtrack of a French thriller."

"Look, change of plan, Dad's not feeling well. Mom doesn't want to drive, so Stephanie's taking them home. Next twenty-two hours, my friend, we've got the boat to ourselves."

Now, The Jewish American Princess had two full-time crew members. Mark tells them they can have the night off. The captain looks concerned, "Are you sure you can handle the boat alone, Boss?" he says. Mark's response is, "I know how to navigate this baby." Before I know it Rhode Island is a thin line on a pretty faraway horizon.

Five miles or so off the coast he throws one anchor off the port side of the boat, a second anchor off the starboard.

"So what am I gonna do with my life, Harry Clarke? I'm thirty-eight years old, man. I'm unfulfilled. I need a change. I need a dirty martini and so do you."

'Round eleven we go below deck. Start to undress. Standing there in nothing but his underwear he announces,

"Let's go up, have a nightcap. So warm!"

Tramps out of the room.

I'm reeling from all the booze.

On deck, he leans over the edge of the boat, balancing a martini. I think for sure he's going to drop overboard. He yells out at the empty sea,

"I like you, Harry Clarke!"

Knocks back the martini, gets a refill from the shaker.

"What makes you special, Harry? My talent is, I know how to make money. What do you think is your gift or your talent or your best attribute?"

"My resilience, my instincts, that's the one thing about myself I always trust, my intuition and, uh…"

"Uh, what?" he says, putting his drink down.

And I can feel myself lighting a match to play with fire.

"What?"

"I'm a little bit psychic."

"Yeah, yeah. I don't believe in that shit. All the 'psychics' setting up shop in New York, such bullshit. So give me an example of your psychic powers."

"Alright."

> *Harry looks to one side as if zoning off into another sphere, looks back at Mark and points.*

"Those boxer briefs, you got them at The Gap in midtown Manhattan. Sixth Avenue and 48th. You bought four packs of two. They were on Special Sale, two packs for twenty dollars."

> *Mark stands back, arms outstretched, aghast.*

"How'd d'you know that? That's incredible. That's fucking amazing! What else can you see with your psychic powers?"

"Oh, I dunno."

"Tell me!"

> *A long, charged pause.*

"I can see me saying to you, I think you should take those boxer briefs off and make your way over here."

"Fucking English. You guys can get away with saying anything! Fucking Harry Clarke. Motherfucker."

He picks up the martini, takes another slurp, puts it down.

"Alright then, and with these psychic powers of yours, what do you see me saying in response?"

"I see you saying, 'You've got the wrong guy.'"

"Then?"

"And me saying, 'You're so predictable.'"

Suddenly he pulls down the boxer briefs and hurls them at me.

"Was that predictable?" he says.

I catch them.

Which in itself is unpredictable.

Philip Brugglestein couldn't catch a ball to save his life, but Harry Clarke could somehow nonchalantly raise his arm in the air and catch a pair of flying underwear from The Gap with effortless grace.

"No, that wasn't predictable. Was this?"

> *Harry hurls the boxer briefs off the side of the boat.*

The boxer briefs float momentarily on the surface of the dark Atlantic Ocean, then disappear out of sight.

> *Long, charged pause.*

"Well, are you gonna come over here, or do I have to come over there and get you?"

> *The lights shift.*

In the car on the way back to New York we don't speak for about eighty miles.

Then he says, "That was a big fuckin' mistake last night, man. A big fucking mistake. I gotta quit drinkin' and if I can't do it on my own I gotta go to A.A."

"Let me ask you a question? Did you have an orgasm?"

> *Mark makes a "I can't believe this question" noise.*

*Harry fixes his eyes on Mark for an answer
and goes on.*

"Was it small, medium or, in the vernacular of your local Starbucks, could it best be described as grande? Venti? ...Dopio? ...Careful, I think we're coming to a toll."

There's no goodbye from Mark as I get out of the car, or if there is I don't hear it.

When I get up to my apartment, I make a beeline for the bathroom. Lean over the toilet, feeling I'm going to throw up, or faint, or both.

To himself.

"What the hell are you doing? You can never do that again. It's a moot point, it's obviously the last you'll ever see of Mark."

Why is it that when I'm myself I'm so fearful all the time? Timid. So wrapped up in what people are thinking about me. But when I'm Harry Clarke I don't give a shit. I'm absolutely, exhilaratingly, alarmingly free.

That was so sexy on the boat. Mama, that was the deep end of sexy.

To himself, as Harry.

"Stick with me kid. I don't have a hang-up in the world."

Lights shift.

This was late June.

Early October I'm walking on the Upper East Side when coming from behind me I hear,

"Harry! Harry!"

First I'm disoriented. I turn 'round, there's a girl with her red hair pulled into a wool cap.

"Stephanie, Mark Schmidt's sister."

As Harry.

"Oh, 'allo."

"What did you do to my crazy brother?"

"What d'you mean?"

"He came back from that weekend with you on the boat, straightaway proposed to this yoga teacher he'd been dating for about a minute. Three weeks later they were married!"

"I didn't know."

"Thought I'd see you at the wedding."

"Guess I wasn't invited."

"You didn't miss anything. It was all his awful macho jock friends."

"Mmm."

"So what are you doing now?"

"Little of this. Little of that. Not too much of anything."

"Hey, I'm singing a new song of mine, a cappella, at the opening of my friend's show tonight at Joe's Pub. I bought a ticket for someone who can't go now, so I have this free ticket. You wanna go? There's just a $12 minimum."

"Thanks, maybe I will. Is Mark going to be there?"

"My crazy brother doesn't come to my shows. Besides, we had a big falling out. So are you gonna come? Come on. Come to my show. Come see my show, Harry Clarke."

Harry grins an "awright, I'll come" grin.

I sit on a stool at Joe's Pub, survey the wall of photos of people who'd performed there in the past – Leonard Cohen, Elvis Costello, Alan Cumming, Adele. Suddenly I think, fuck, you better check the wall for Sade. If she's performed at Joe's Pub, you should know about it.

But Sade is nowhere to be seen.

Stephanie walks out on stage, a light comes up on her, and she starts to sing.

Stephanie sings an original, bluesy song, "Wide Back Boy."

"I WANNA WIDE BACK BOY
GIMME A WIDE BACK BOY
I WANT A DIFFERENT KIND OF LOVE
I WANNA FIND MY JOY
WANNA LOSE MY GRIP
WAKE MY HIPS
WANNA DO SOME THINGS I NEVER DONE BEFORE

GIMME A WIDE BACK BOY
A WITTY WIDE BACK BOY
WITH A SPARKLE IN HIS EYE
IT'S GONNA LIGHT THE LIGHT INSIDE ME
WANNA LOSE MY HEAD
LAUGH IN BED
DO SOME THINGS I NEVER DONE BEFORE

I'M SO TIRED OF FEELIN' KINDA LONELY
I'M SO TIRED OF FEELIN' KIND OF BLUE
I'M SO TIRED OF WAKIN' UP ALONE EACH DAY
I WANNA SAY TO LONELINESS,
'HEY, FUCK YOU!'
I GOT A WIDE BACK BOY
A PRETTY WIDE BACK BOY
WITH A WILD IMAGINATION
LORD, HE TREATS ME LIKE A PLAY THING
GONNA LOSE OUR GRIP
SAIL THIS SHIP
DO SOME THINGS WE NEVER DONE BEFORE

I'M GONNA DO SOME THINGS I NEVER DONE BEFORE
WANNA DO SOME THINGS I NEVER DONE BEFORE

WHERE'S MY WIDE BACK BOY?"

    The song ends.

After the show Stephanie invites me to a diner with her for apple pie.

Mid-pie she says to me, "I'm sure my brother is gay. Drives me crazy he won't get over his machismo and admit it to himself. Particularly since our dad died."

"I'm sorry. I didn't know."

"Well, our father was very homophobic. Mark, years ago, had this older friend, Michael, who he was so obviously in love with. It's funny, when I first met you I thought, oh my God, that guy looks so much like Michael. Except you're not blond. Michael, even though he was receding, one day decided to dye his hair trashy blond."

"Trashy blond?"

"Yeah, you know that overtly peroxide look where the dark roots deliberately show. He and Mark were going to produce movies together, but he died suddenly, some undetected bone marrow disease, and Mark was...you couldn't get near him. He was inconsolable.

Then he made this grand show of going from one bimbo girl to another, finally careening into the evil Sabine, who I'm sure just married him so she could get a green card. Now this yoga teacher, Lexie. Oh my God, is this girl boring. Walks in a room and sucks the air out of it. I'm such a bitch.

Our father's will left Mark very comfortably off. My point being, my brother doesn't need to work anymore, which is really the worst thing for him. He spends all his time now going to the gym and, from what I hear, doing a tremendous amount of cocaine, and God knows what else. You know he always had an issue with drugs. He's been in and out of treatment since he was seventeen."

I walk her to the subway. She kisses me on the lips. First I can't tell if it's a kiss, kiss or a kiss goodnight. A second kiss makes the picture clearer.

    She pulls away.

"I shouldn't do this, I live with someone. I'm sorry. Hey, thanks for coming to the gig. Appreciate it."

I write down HARRY CLARKE and my number on the show's program. Hand it to her.

"If you ever need a break from your boyfriend, gimme a call."

"It's nice to be offered temptation."

"Everyone should be offered temptation at least once a month. Keeps a spring in your step."

"I'll remember that."

"Hey, there's no expiration date on the offer."

"I'll remember that too."

She heads down the steps of the subway, then turns back around,

"I'm feeling neglected. Do you have a mint, and a place to go?"

"Got a place to go, but I can't supply the mint."

"I drank an espresso before the show, I think I need a mint."

She ducks into Walgreens.

I stand on the sidewalk outside thinking, what the hell are you doing? You cannot take her to your apartment. There's a Philip Brugglestein Con Edison bill on the table. A Philip Brugglestein AT&T bill.

To himself, as Harry.

"Don't get your knickers in a twist, darling."

We cab it uptown.

In the entrance of my building Stephanie glances at the door buzzers.

"Which one are you?"

"Four B"

"Who's Philip Brugglestein?"

"Guy I sublet the place from."

In the apartment she makes a beeline for the DVDs.

"Somebody likes movies."

"They're Philip's."

"I've never seen so many film noirs and thrillers."

"I don't think he has much of a life."

"Is that a phone answering machine? Haven't seen one of those in years. Is that a phone from the 1920s attached to it?"

> *This question prompts a momentary flicker of Philip to come out in response.*

"1941."

"Wow, fits right in with the movies."

She takes off her coat, checks her watch.

"Okay, we've got forty-five minutes."

"What if I want to go into overtime?"

"If we go into overtime, my 'union' will come down on me heavily, so no going over."

We go to kiss and the kiss is interrupted by the sounds of a trilling canary coming out of her pocket.

"My phone. Forgot to turn it off. It's home, probably calling to see where I am. I'm sorry. I should go. This isn't the answer to my feelings of ambivalence."

She picks up her coat.

"Remember, there's no sell-by date on the offer."

Grins, then she's gone.

> *Lights shift.*

I needed cash. The money I'd gotten from selling my dad's house had run to almost nothing.

Pick up a job as a barista in a Madison Avenue pastry cafe. Life returns to the unimaginative and the demeaning.

I get treated slightly better than the other people working there because I have an English accent. La Cappuccine is a real watering hole for snobs. Snobs and models and over-caffeinated ladies who lunch who only really engaged with me when they wanted recommendations of places to go, and sights to see, in London – a town I'd never been to in my life.

I'm spending most of my spare time on my own and I find myself reflecting too much.

Descending into some kind of Indiana haze.

I think about my father's funeral, and my father's friend Will Horstman berating me.

"Philip, you knew your father was a severe alcoholic, and taking the tractor out at night in such an inebriated state was just calling for an accident. You should have stopped him."

And my responding, "Maybe if he didn't call me 'faggot' every five minutes I would have tried!"

I think about that night, what a pig my father was being.

"Every kid in the neighborhood wants to sit on my tractor, but my kid? My kid just wants to pansy around with a faggoty English accent. Ey, what's wrong with you? Ey? Ey? Ey?"

Slapping my head. Pinning me up against a wall. And Harry Clarke rearing up, grabbing him by the throat, yelling, "Chill out, you small minded, ignorant motherfucker!"

"What, you're a goddamn Cockney now?"

"You need a stiff drink."

"I've been on the wagon for three months!"

"Well, sweetheart, it's time to get off! Sit down, I'm gonna fix you a drink."

My father knocking back a rye whisky, and another, and another.

Harry Clarke saying, "Well aren't you gonna give me a driving lesson."

Him staggering out the back door.

Hearing him start the engine, lose his balance and fall forward into the path of the moving tractor. How his last word on this earth was half a word – "Motherfff!" The sound of the unmanned tractor smashing into the neighbor's car, and Harry Clarke saying, "Just go to bed, go to sleep, you were asleep when it happened."

The police officer waking me up and saying, "Phil, there's been a terrible accident."

And all I could think as the police officer looked sympathetically at me was, oh my God, you have the most beautiful eyes. Tell everyone to go home, and come to bed.

And as the ambulance took my dad's body away feeling absolutely nothing, except fascination for the paleness of that young cop's blue eyes.

I always thought the stress of living with my dad caused the cancer that killed my mother, but that was all in the past. The present is the tedium of La Cappuccine, and struggling to make ends meet in New York.

When it comes to work, I have no skills. I'm not much use to anyone.

One night in the apartment I yell out in frustration,

"I'm so sick of my life! All my friends have drifted away. All I do is work. I need a change! I need a fucking change!"

And as my poor mother used to say,

"From your mouth to God's ears."

I'm lying in bed. One o'clock in the morning, phone rings. I'm thinking, who the hell's calling me at this hour?

Machine picks up, and I hear,

> *Sounding stoned and drunk.*

"Harry! Hey, it's Mark Schmidt. Been meaning to call you, man. Lot of crazy stuff to tell. I got married. Total fucking mistake. I broke it off. She moved out. Bought a new apartment, I'm having it renovated, so I'm staying at the Paramount Hotel for a few weeks. You want to come over and hang out in the room? Room 615. Come over man, any time. Don't be afraid of waking me up. I want to see you!"

Pulled the covers over me, thinking "don't go." Eventually fell asleep.

In the morning I replay the message, and Harry Clarke kicks in,

"I think we should get our hair dyed trashy blond, pay a little visit to Room 615, and just see what happens."

Next thing I'm on the phone.

"'Allo, I'd like to get my hair dyed blond. What's the earliest you could do it?

> *Again he re-counts the story, re-telling only his side of the conversation.*

You had a cancellation?

Yeah, I could be there at eleven.

Clarke, with an E.

Thank you."

And when I hang up I realize I've just made an appointment under Harry's name.

Before I can think about it too much I'm sitting in a salon explaining to a colorist exactly what I mean by trashy blond.

I had a shift from four to ten that evening at La Cappuccine. I'm standing behind the counter when the manager signals me.

> *He imitates the manager signalling him over and speaking.*

"Philip, you can't work here looking like that. I'm going to have to let you go."

Harry Clarke rears up.

"This is bullshit. If I was a girl and went blond I'd be swimming in a sea of compliments. And what about you? With your boot polish black dye job."

There is something oddly therapeutic about being physically thrown out of a place you hated working in.

Eleven o'clock that evening I'm standing outside the Paramount Hotel, taking in the irony of being back at the place where I'd first followed Mark to.

Slip into the men's room on the ground floor. Look into my own eyes reflected in the mirrored walls and Harry Clarke has a heart-to-heart with me.

"I think the dramatic change you're looking for is standing right in front of you. Hello, pleased to meet you. I'm your new life. Give me three months where you're only me. A trial offer, shall we say."

Aping a commercial.

"Be Harry Clarke for ninety days, and if you're not completely satisfied..."

Back to normal voice.

"Your life's like a broken record. It's time to shatter the tune. Be me for three months and see what happens. Go on. Give it a whirl."

Lights shift.

From this point the story is told by Harry Clarke.

Next thing I'm moseying through the lobby of the Paramount Hotel, with, shall we say, the confidence of a guest. Call out to the desk clerk, "Goodnight, Luv." Elevator up to room 615.

Mark opens the door wearing sweatpants and a Mets T-shirt.

"Harry! I'm so happy to see you, man."

And I'm thinking, who is this skinny guy hugging me hello? Before, Mark had a bit of a belly. Belly is gone. He's lean and gym-ified. And when I get all the way in the room, I pull off the woolen hat I have on, give him the big reveal.

"You're blond!"

"Needed to shake things up a bit."

"Oh my God Harry, you look so much like my friend Michael, who died!"

"Oh really?"

"It's unbelievable, man."

He crumples onto the bed.

"I think some people that come into your life are a kind of test run for someone who'll come into your life later. Am I making sense? Shit, I've had too much ecstasy. Man, I think there's something meant to be about the two of us. What do you think? Tell me, what do you think?"

"I'll tell you what I think. I think I was thinking the same thing as I was just walking into the hotel.

I think it's very nice to see you.

I think you look rather dishy in that ripped at the collar Mets T-shirt.

I think I don't miss your little belly at all.

I think I should flip that Do Not Disturb sign to the other side of the door.

I think you should fix us a drink from that no-doubt exorbitantly priced hotel room bar.

I think we got some making up to do."

Three days later I waltz out of Room 615 thinking, Gordon Bennett, what have I unleashed. He's like a bloody rabbit. A rabbit that does a lot of ecstasy. The old twigs and berries got a real workout.

I've gone three blocks when I get a text –

I MISS YOU!

Another ten blocks, second text pops up –

HEY MAN, DON'T TELL ANYONE ABOUT US. OUR SECRET, OKAY?

I text back –

OK.

In the apartment I put some music on and stare into the mirror.

>*We hear the track Harry has selected.*[*]
>
>*It's a romantic movie composition that might underscore a love scene.*
>
>*Philip as Harry speaks over the movie music, all the while looking in the mirror, trying out lines.*

"Fuck you, Mark. I'm starting to fall in love with you."

"I think I'm a little bit in love with you."

No, that's awful.

"I'm sticking my neck out by saying this. Don't look at me like that! I think I'm falling for you."

"I've got such a crush on you. Alright, I'll just say it. Hey Mark, I'm in love with you."

"I'm in love with you, ya dope."

"I feel uncharacteristically vulnerable right now."

"Mark, I love you. I love you, Mark."

No, not sexy.

"You fucking arsehole, I'm falling in love with you."

"I've never quite felt like this before."

"I can't stop thinking about you. You're like an obsession. The way you taste. The way you look. Watching you sleep, I'm so full of feeling. I think I'm going to burst."

"I'm fucking falling in love with you, Mark Schmidt. I'm falling in love with you."

---

*A license to produce *Harry Clarke* does not include a performance license for any third-party or copyrighted underscoring music. Licensees should create an original composition or use music in the public domain. For further information, please see Music Use Note on page iii.

Yeah, that's the best one – "I'm fucking falling in love with you, Mark Schmidt."

The music track ends.

Mark's new place is a stunning loft on Lafayette Street. I'm spending most of my time there.

On the one hand he says I should move a load of my clothes in. On the other he's terrified people'll put two and two together. That we're havin' it off. When anyone comes over, all my stuff gets bundled into a closet, and I go for a walk or go uptown or go see a movie. It's annoying and tiresome and kinda sexy. Bein' someone's secret life.

I meet some of these so-called friends. Bunch of privileged wankers whose only money worries in life are what to do with it all. I'm not blowing my own horn, but alongside these tossers, I can see why he's enamored of me.

After a few months of bein' in the orbit of moneyed jocks and the steel-eyed birds that go for that sort of thing, I'm gettin' bored. Need to have a little bit of fun.

Mark's mum, Ruth, who I did have a soft spot for, had moved from Maine to a house in Cherry Hill, New Jersey, after the old man died. I says to Mark, "Curiously, I have to go to Cherry Hill to meet a music biz guy. Why don't I call your mum when I'm out there."

"Oh, man, my mom would be over the moon. She's so smitten with you."

So I give Ruth a tinkle.

"'Allo, love, you up for a visit?"

"Harry! Yes! Come over!"

So I go over to her house. The place has a giant garden that's secluded from the other houses. It's warm and sunny. She's sittin' on the patio with two bottles of Sauvignon Blanc. One of 'em empty. The Schmidts could really knock it back.

We're sittin' out there for a couple of hours. Yacking. I'm in a state of semi-captivation over the size of her hair. Thinkin', how d'you get it to do that? She's gettin' pretty sloshed.

"I could just listen to your voice all day, Harry. I love British accents."

"So, are you datin' anyone, Ruth?"

"God, Honey I wish. I'm sixty-seven years old, for chrissakes, I'm not a hundred and seven! Harry, I'll be frank with you. Some days I sit around here thinking, am I ever gonna have sex again? Oh, Harry, I don't like guys my age. It's a problem. I should move to your country. I'm so crazy about all things British. All I do all day is watch British TV, and drink."

"Ruth, I was just thinkin'. Shall we have a one-off, bonding moment, that's just between you and me?"

"A secret? Harry, I love it! What?"

"Ruth, would you like to suck my cock?"

"Aaaaah! What here? On the patio?"

"No one can see. Your garden's completely bushed off."

"You're my kid's friend."

"This is nothin' to do with Mark. It's between you and me."

"Harry, I have never been propositioned like that in my life."

"That's how we roll in London. We desire something, we go for it. Well?"

> *She considers.*

"You're not uncircumcised are you? No offence to people who are uncircumcised, but I'm Jewish, Harry. I mean, I'm not Orthodox or anything. But I don't think I could put an uncircumcised penis in my mouth. I think I would gag. I can't eat shrimp either."

> *Ruth makes a flabbergasted gasping sound that also suggests she's game.*

When I get back to the apartment Mark says, "How was it with my mom?"

"Oh, we had the best visit."

"Thanks for doing that, Harry."

"It was my treat, really. She gave me a lot of pleasure. Really extended herself to me. In fact I would say she almost overextended herself."

He puts his arms around me says, "I love that you're having a whole thing with my mom. That just makes me feel even closer to you. She never liked any of the girls I dated."

He kisses me, and there's something different about it.

We're huggin' and kissin'. It's very sweet.

Afterwards we're sprawled out on the bed.

"I never wanted to lay around with a girl. I could lay around with you all day. This is gonna sound corny, Harry, but laying around with you, I feel like I'm home."

"I feel the same way. It's just comforting to have no clothes on with you. To lie around. Hold you."

"I think it takes a lot of guts to be open about yourself. I feel like I'm gettin' closer to being ready for it. What have I been doing? Was always whenever anyone would talk about gay people in front of me I would clench up inside and wait for the subject to change. Man, I wish there was a better word than 'gay.' I don't like the word 'gay.'"

"Yeah, it's not very sexy. I don't like it either. Anyway, why do you have to give everything a label. You are what you are with the girls, and you are what you are with me. I am what I am with the girls. I am what I am with you."

We lay there.

"What are you thinking?"

"No, I was just thinkin' about you, I think you're much more artistic than you know, and you should produce a movie which will allow all your latent artistic gifts to see the light of day. That's what I'm thinkin'."

"I should produce a movie with you, Harry. We should produce a movie together."

He sits bolt upright on the bed.

"Harry, we should make a movie!"

And I'm thinkin', Bingo!

And Mark gets on it. Calls around to all the writers agencies. Asks them to send him scripts for a low-budget movie he would be producing, and all these screenplays start showing up at the door.

All of 'em are bloody awful.

"This is all a bunch of codswallop," I tell him. "You should write your own."

So he starts to try to write a film script about his childhood relationship with his reclusive grandfather who'd survived the Nazis.

It was a beautiful story. And the funny thing was, Mark could write, and my comments on the script as it was coming along, if I do say so myself, were rather on the mark.

I think, that's what I am. Harry Clarke is a man who makes movies.

And it's all systems go there, for a bit.

Whole thing goes awry when Mark starts researching writers he admired, finds they have one thing in common, they all were drunk when they wrote their best work, which gives him license to start drinking from the moment he gets out of bed. Between this and the speed he's taking so he can work into the night, and the ubiquitous cocaine. Some nights I feel like the ringmaster of a three-ring circus.

"I want you to lay off the drugs," is what I say to him in the living room. "I don't think we're ever gonna get a movie made unless you do. It's making you crazy, and what am I going to do if you accidentally o.d.?"

Mark rages.

"Don't you ever tell me that I shouldn't drink, or do drugs, or smoke a joint, or do a line of coke. Ever. You understand me? I like cocaine, and if I want to do cocaine, I'm gonna do cocaine. Do you understand? Don't want to hear this shit ever again! You're in my world now. You understand? You get it?"

And that was the moment I saw a side of Mark I haven't seen up to this point.

I go up on the roof. Think, this guy's a spoiled rich brat who's turning into a junkie. I gotta get outta this. Then I think, whoah, whoah, whoah, eyes on the road, Harry. Eyes on the road.

After Mark sleeps it off, he's all apologies. But I can feel the reality of the film ever happening slipping away quickly.

One night Mark's erratic behavior is driving me up the bloody wall. Take myself to the movies. I'm comin' out of the cinema when I get an unexpected phone call.

"Harry. Hey, it's Stephanie Schmidt."

"Oh, 'allo."

"I'll get straight to the point, Harry. Is that offer of temptation still good?"

"Yeah, it is. When d'you want to be tempted?"

"How about right now?"

"Where are you?"

In the apartment we jump in where we'd left off.

"You are a sexy, fucking girl."

"Harry, you don't know how much I needed to hear that. I'm living with a guy I love, who is perpetually depressed and right now if I touch him he flinches like I've given him an electric shock."

"Wanna do some things you've never done before?"

"You remembered!"

"I'm hardly a wide back boy, but I'll give it a go."

Lead her to the bed, pull up her dress.

Stephanie Schmidt is not the kind of girl who buys her underwear at The Gap.

"Nice knickers," I say as I pull 'em down and throw 'em on the floor. "That is the most immaculate looking Brazilian wax I've ever seen."

"It was a Hanukkah present from my girlfriends at work."

"Thank you, 'girlfriends at work.' Thank you very,

very,

very

much."

Two hours later I put Stephanie in a cab back to her life, and I get in another cab and go down to Lafayette.

Mark is asleep when I walk in. I breathe in his ear.

"Wake up. Wake up."

"You smell of the perfume my sister always wears."

"My friend I went to the movie with wears a lot of perfume. I want to make love to you."

"I'm asleep."

"I can't stop thinking about you. You're like an obsession. The way you taste. The way you look. Watching you sleep just now, I'm so full of feeling. I think I'm gonna burst. You know what one of my favorite things to do is? Pullin' your knickers down and chuckin' 'em across the room. Just like this.

He gestures tossing the underwear.

"Come on.

Come on.

Come on."

But the cocaine binges are really getting under my skin. They're making him incredibly paranoid. So I start keeping a journal, which I know he's reading. So I begin catering to my audience. Writing about the minutiae of our relationship and telling him things he wants to hear.

Then it comes to me –

I'm gonna have a will drawn up and leave everything to Mark. The "flat in London" that I told him I had. The contents of the studio uptown. Whatever there is of mine in his apartment. The whole kit and kaboodle. Find a lawyer to draw up a draft that I have no intention of signing. Leave the draft in an envelope sticking out the side of my bag.

I come in one day. Mark's all emotional.

He says, "I got to confess I went through your bag and opened that envelope. I read your will and I'm so moved."

"I don't have much, but 'course I'm gonna leave everything to you."

Then comes the night where he decides that he should get so drunk that he'll make himself so ill that he'll never want to touch a drink again. The evening climaxes with him screaming at me and stumbling into a standard lamp which goes smashing into my face. Split my nose open. Could see the bloody bone. I say, "I'm leaving," and I walk out on him.

And every strung out sounding phone message he leaves for me, goes unreturned.

Philip returns to his regular speaking voice.

I cut the blond out of my hair, flush it down the toilet and that Harry Clarke period of my life draws to a close. Things go back to the way they were. I'm back to treading the pavements, trying to get a job.

Five months goes by, I think, I can't afford to stay in New York anymore. Can't get work. Don't know what I'm going to do, or where I'm going to go. I come home, there's a message on my answering machine.

"Mr. Clarke, my name is Brad Gould, I'm the lawyer representing the estate of the late Mark Schmidt. Can you please call me at your earliest convenience. My number at the office is…"

I'm thinkin', the late Mark Schmidt?

So I call this Brad Gould.

"I assumed you knew, Mr. Clarke. I'm sorry to have to be the bearer of this news. Mr. Schmidt was on his way to a rehab facility in North Carolina, when he suffered a heart attack. He died about two months ago, and you are the sole beneficiary of the will. But Mr. Clarke I think I should also tell you the family's attorney has advised them to contest the validity of the will. As Mr. Schmidt had a well-documented drug history, they feel he didn't have his full faculties when the will was drawn. And there is an additional factor that all the money from the recent sale of the family's boat, The Jewish American Princess, had not yet been distributed. A third each to Stephanie and her mother, but remained in Mark's accounts."

"Can I call you back? I'm in shock, hearing about Mark's death."

I hang up, and I think, will you cry. Just cry!

I call back.

"How much is the estate worth?"

"With all the assets combined, including revenue from the sale of the boat, and the estimated value of the Lafayette Street apartment, the estate is valued somewhere in the region of eleven to twelve million dollars."

I hang up and fly into panic mode.

I cannot take this money. It's blood money. And besides, there's no such person as Harry Clarke!

> *To himself, as Harry.*

But there could be. Look, you got no money. You can't get work. You gonna move back to South Bend, Indiana Philip Brugglestein? What you gonna do? Get a job waiting tables in Olive Garden? Red Lobster? Filling up the shelves in Walmart? You do need me.

You should legally change your name to Harry Clarke. This will stuff is going to take a while to sort out. Meanwhile, you'll get your name change.

Let me go back to the lawyer that drew up the Harry Clarke will.

I'll tell him that I'm the sole inheritor of a substantial amount of money from my friend, who may not have been in his right mind when he made up his will, and for the sake of fairness, I want to re-write the will, as a gesture of goodwill. And one that has the potential of heading off some aggressive legal action on the part of the Schmidt family.

> *Back to Philip's voice.*

And this is what we do.

Ryan, my lawyer, proposes to liquidate the estate and do a three-way even split. Ruth and Stephanie agree to it. We all come in and sign. Ruth's wearing big dark glasses.

On the street outside the estate lawyer's office Stephanie comes up to me,

"Why did my brother leave everything he had to you?"

> *As he interacts with Stephanie and Ryan, he speaks as Harry.*

"I dunno."

"Were you fucking my brother?"

I don't say anything.

She slaps me across the face.

"I thought people only did that in movies."

She walks away.

Lawyer Ryan asks me what I was going to do now the inheritance has been settled.

"I'm gonna go to England. I've never been."

He laughs.

"I'm going to an exotic island and just sit on the beach."

Speaking as Philip with his English accent.

I fall in love with the Seychelle Islands the moment I step off the plane. Feel it in my gut, this is where I'm supposed to be.

First night in the villa I open up my passport. Stare at the photo and the words "Harry Edward Clarke." Put the Edward in because I always liked the name.

Besides, Philip Brugglestein was such a mouthful. You were always having to spell it.

And I mean really, it's your life. Least you should be able to do is choose your own name.

I go to the bathroom. Stare at my reflection.

Speaking as Philip with his American accent.

Alright, I give up. You got me. Who are you?

You look a bit like your father, but you're not your father. You look a bit like your mother, but you're not your mother. Who are you?

He stares into the mirror without answering.

He crosses to the deck chair and sits.

Laying out in a deck chair, looking at the Indian Ocean, you can feel yourself coming back to yourself. All the disparate pieces of your personality, settling into one.

This sweet girl from the villa comes over and says, "Mr. Clarke, can I bring you another drink?"

"No, thank you. And please call me Harry. But can you put my music back on. Just press 'play.'"

> *We hear haunting cinematic music, the kind that might play at the end of a movie.**
>
> *Philip speaks over it.*

I did end up going to England. London. I didn't really like it. Didn't like that everyone sounded kinda like me.

> *Philip speaking as Harry.*

And it rained the whole bloody time!

> *Harry grins.*
>
> *The music plays.*
>
> *The lights fade.*

---

*A license to produce *Harry Clarke* does not include a performance license for any third-party or copyrighted cinematic music. Licensees should create an original composition or use music in the public domain. For further information, please see Music Use Note on page iii.

Harry Clarke

Music and Lyrics
David Cale

Condom in Your Car

I found a con - dom in your car.   I found a con - dom in your car.

I found a con - dom in your car.   So yes it's   o - ver.

Music and Lyrics
David Cale

Wide Back Boy

I'm so tired of feel - in' kind - a lone-ly.

I'm so tired of feel - in' kind - a blue.

I'm so tired of wak - ing up a - lone each day. I

wan - na say to lone - li - ness, "Hey, fuck you!" I got - ta

wide back boy a pret-ty wide back boy. With a

wild i - mag - in - a - tion, Lord he

treats me like a play thing. Gon - na lose

our grip. Sail this ship. Do

some things we've ne - ver done be - fore.

Wide back boy! Wide back boy!

Bring me joy. Find— the life in - side me— Gon-na

lose my grip! Sail my ship! Do

— some things I've ne-ver done be - fore. I'm gon-na

do some things I've ne-ver done be - fore. I'm gon-na

do some-things I've ne - ver done be - fore.

Where's my wide back boy?

Milton Keynes UK
Ingram Content Group UK Ltd.
UKHW030128070324
438984UK00010BA/164

9 780573 707308